Everybody, Everybody

Everybody, Everybody

A COLLECTION FROM
The Paper Bag Players

BY

Judith Martin

MUSIC BY

Donald Ashwander

ILLUSTRATED BY

Gary Ciccati

ELSEVIER / NELSON BOOKS
New York

No character in these plays is intended to represent any actual person.

Library of Congress Cataloging in Publication Data
Martin, Judith.
    Everybody, everybody.

    Contents: Everybody, everybody—The chicken and the egg—
The building and the statute—[etc.]
    1. Children's plays, American. [1. Plays] I. Ciccati,
Gary, ill. II. Ashwander, Donald. III. Title.
PS3563.A237E93   812'.54   81–9899
ISBN 0–525–66736–9   AACR2
Published in the United States by E. P. Dutton, Inc., 2 Park Avenue, New York, N.Y. 10016.
Published simultaneously in Canada by Clarke, Irwin & Company Limited, Toronto and Vancouver
Editor: Virginia Buckley   Designer: Trish Parcell
Printed in the U.S.A.   First edition
10 9 8 7 6 5 4 3 2 1

Acknowledgments

Since its formation in 1958, The Paper Bag Players has been my artistic home. I will always feel indebted to my performing friends who helped create and sustain it. I do not know of any other theater where the various members have each played such an important role.

Throughout the years Irving Burton, featured player of The Paper Bag Players, has been a mainstay of the company. His ability to give physical reality to the vaguest idea and conviction to the most farfetched characters has often been crucial in getting the plays from rehearsal studio to stage. Together with Donald Ashwander and me he has been central in creating the last seven shows.

The founding of the company as well as the first plays would not have been possible without the daring imaginations of Remy Charlip and Shirley Kaplan. Sudie Bond and Daniel Jahn, then members of the group, gave generously of their time and talent. Betty Osgood joined the company soon after it was formed and brought to it an amazing presence and a unique sense of comedy. With Donald Ashwander the company found its musical personality.

Because The Paper Bag Plays evolve in rehearsal, they are frequently the expression of several people's imaginations. In the excitement of rehearsals one person's contributions are hard to separate from another's. The list given here, based on memories of rehearsals and old program notes, is an attempt to give credit to the main contributors to each play. All the music is by Donald Ashwander.

EVERYBODY, EVERYBODY: Judith Martin, Donald Ashwander, Douglas Norwick, Irving Burton

THE CHICKEN AND THE EGG: Judy Martin, Remy Charlip, Shirley Kaplan, Betty Osgood

THE BUILDING AND THE STATUE: Remy Charlip, Judy Martin, Shirley Kaplan, Betty Osgood

BLOWN OFF THE BILLBOARD: Judy Martin, Irving Burton

MA AND THE KIDS: Judy Martin, Irving Burton, Remy Charlip

THAT'S GOOD, THAT'S GOOD: Judy Martin, Donald Ashwander

BIG BURGER: Judy Martin

I WON'T TAKE A BATH!: Judy Martin

The music accompanying these plays
will be found following page 77.

Contents

Introduction

For several years after leaving professional theater school I earned my living teaching children's classes in drama and dance. The children who took these classes did not aspire to stage careers. They came mainly for the fun of it, craving the personal expression and excitement associated with theater. To satisfy this craving I found myself constantly pressed to invent stories, plays, and dramatic games. When some friends and I formed The Paper Bag Players, these stories were the basis of our first shows.

All the plays in this book come from shows produced by The Paper Bag Players. They can be performed separately or combined into a presentation that takes about one hour. These plays are meant for people who simply would like to "put on a show." Most children's groups that present plays do not have formal casting. Since everyone usually wants a part, the plays in this collection have expandable casts. For instance, there can be many eggs and chickens in "The Chicken and the Egg."

Ordinary materials—paper bags and cardboard boxes—become imaginative costumes and props that are easy to make and very inexpensive. Grocery and liquor stores, furniture and appliance shops, and department-store loading platforms are all good sources for boxes.

Music, which is an integral part of The Paper Bag Plays, is written here in a simple form so that a moderately trained piano player can perform it. Dancing can be incorporated into several of the plays, and popular dance works as well as modern and ballet.

In our company, actors on stage call each other by their first names. We suggest that other groups use their actors' own first names, for it gives the performance a warm and friendly feeling.

From the start, the work of The Paper Bag Players has taken its inspiration from the imaginations of children. We are very pleased that our plays are now available in print for children themselves to produce.

Judith Martin

Everybody, Everybody

PROPS

2 plastic milk crates
1 cardboard box, table height
4 cardboards, 29 inches
  wide by 36 inches high
1 large paper bag, about 36
  inches high
straw hat for JEANNE
sun hat for IRVING
paper plate with cardboard knife
and fork attached, wrapped in
  paper napkin
1 paper chicken, made of
  stuffed paper bag, with paper
  chicken legs attached with
  Velcro or tape
1 pair cardboard boxing gloves
1 book

PRODUCTION NOTES

The four cardboard pieces should extend from each actor's neck to his knees. Each cardboard has a painted torso on it. There is a fat woman, a thin woman, a fat man, and a thin man. The fat woman has a thin woman painted on the back. These cardboards are also used as tabletops in the picnic scene.
The boxing gloves are stuffed paper bags with elastic at wrists.

CAST

JUDY   DOUG
IRVING   JEANNE
DONALD (pianist)

Everybody, Everybody

Action music. The actors run onstage carrying props needed in the skits. They set their props down at side of stage. Music ends.

(JUDY *shakes hands with* IRVING. IRVING *kisses* JUDY *on the cheek.)*

Judy   Irving, this kissing business embarrasses me.

Irving   But shaking hands is so cold and formal.

Judy   I was taught to shake hands with my friends.

Irving   And I was taught to kiss my friends.

Judy   Okay, Irving, forget it.

Irving   Okay.

Judy Say, do you want to come to my house for dinner tonight?

Irving Sure, Judy. What are you having?

Judy We're having a special treat—rattlesnake steak!

Irving Rattlesnake steak! You'd better come to *my* house for dinner.

Judy Okay, what are you having?

Irving Pigs' ears!

Judy Pigs' ears? Where did you ever learn to eat pigs' ears?

Irving In my family, we've been eating pigs' ears for years.

Judy Pigs' ears for years? I was taught to stay away from pigs' ears.

Irving And I was taught to stay away from rattlesnake steak.

Judy Irving, you know what my mother used to say about things like that? "Everybody, everybody, everybody, everybody, everybody thinks they're doing it right."

(DOUG *and* JEANNE, *standing on the side of the stage, have been listening. Now* DOUG *sings and circles around*

6

JUDY *and* IRVING. *As* DOUG *sings, he does a simple dance step and, holding his arms in front of his chest, rolls his hands around each other in time with the music.)*

Doug
Everybody, Everybody, Everybody, Everybody,
Everybody thinks they're doing it right.

Everybody, Everybody, Everybody, Everybody,
Everybody thinks they're doing it right.

Judy Doug, did you just make up that song?

Doug No.

Irving I never heard that song.

Doug Oh, that's an old song. Donald knows that song.

Donald I don't know that song.

Doug But, Donald, you're playing that song.

Donald I can play it but I don't know it.

Doug He's only kidding, and when we sing that song we always do this.

(He repeats dance step and hand rolling and sings.)

Doug
Everybody, Everybody, Everybody, Everybody,
Everybody thinks they're doing it right.

(JUDY *and* IRVING *sing the song with* DOUG. *They all join the dance step and roll their hands.*)

Everybody, Everybody, Everybody, Everybody, Everybody thinks they're doing it right.

Judy Douglas, I know you must have just made up that song.

(JEANNE *comes forward and sings the song. She also does the dance step and hand rolling.*)

Jeanne
Everybody, Everybody, Everybody, Everybody, Everybody thinks they're doing it right.

Everybody, Everybody, Everybody, Everybody, Everybody thinks they're doing it right.

Doug You see, Judy, I didn't just make up that song.

Irving Jeanne, when did you learn that song? Didn't you just hear Doug sing it?

Jeanne Why, I've always known that song. Everybody knows that song. (*To audience*) You know that song, don't you?

Jeanne (*Audience responds Yes and No.*) You see, everybody knows that song.

Judy   Jeanne, I heard a lot of people out there say No.

Jeanne   Well, I heard a lot of people say Yes.

Judy   A lot of people is not everybody.

Irving   Why argue when we can sing? (*To audience*) Even if you don't know that song, let's all sing that song.

(The actors sing with audience and perform dance step. Many of the audience do hand movements in their seats.)

All

Everybody, Everybody, Everybody, Everybody, Everybody thinks they're doing it right.

Everybody, Everybody, Everybody, Everybody, Everybody thinks they're doing it right.

The cast sets up for the next skit. One box with cardboard pieces on top becomes a table. Two milk crates on either side are chairs for IRVING *and* JEANNE. DOUG *takes a large paper bag from a pile of props and places it near the table.* JUDY *hands* IRVING *and* JEANNE *hats from the paper bag.* JUDY *and* DOUG *look on as* IRVING *and* JEANNE *begin the next skit.*

The Picnic

Irving Jeanne, everybody does think they're doing it right.

Jeanne Yes, they do, Irving.

Irving Let's eat.

Jeanne Okay.

Irving Here's your lunch all wrapped up because I know you're so fussy.

(IRVING *takes paper plate wrapped in white paper napkin from the big bag and gives it to* JEANNE.)

Jeanne I'm not fussy, Irving. I just believe in good manners.

Irving Well, I don't worry about things like that.

(IRVING *takes a whole paper chicken out of large bag. He tears the legs off, chomps at one of them, and bites into chicken's body.* JEANNE *eats delicately with knife and fork. She offers* IRVING *a paper napkin. He tosses it away.* JEANNE *grabs his chicken and tosses it into the bag.* IRVING *throws her plate into bag.* JEANNE *throws her hat into bag.* IRVING *tosses his hat into bag.*)

10

Jeanne Irving!

Irving Jeanne!

Doug Jeanne!

Judy Irving!

Doug Remember that song?

Jeanne What song?

Doug That song.

Irving The song you made up.

Doug I did not make up that song.

Jeanne That's the song everybody knows.

Judy Everybody does not know that song.

Irving Why argue when we can all sing that song?

(All actors do dance step and rolling hand movement.)

All
Everybody, Everybody, Everybody, Everybody,
Everybody thinks they're doing it right.

Everybody, Everybody, Everybody, Everybody,
Everybody thinks they're doing it right.

Irving (*To* JEANNE) To show you I'm not mad, I'll use
your napkin.

11

(Gets napkin from bag and delicately wipes his mouth.)

Jeanne   Irving, to show you I'm not mad, I'll take a bite of your chicken.

(Gets chicken from bag and bites into it.)

Jeanne   Ummmm, that's good.

(Action music. The actors pick up props and move them offstage. They are ready for the next skit. Music ends.)

Fat and Thin

Judy   *(To audience)* People argue about all sorts of things, not only about how to eat, but what to eat, and how much to eat. Now I firmly believe that one should eat to make oneself happy.

(DOUG places cardboard with a picture of a fat body in front of JUDY.)

Judy   *(Walking downstage)* Which reminds me—I'm in the mood for a great big plate of spaghetti.

(JEANNE *takes from the pile of props a cardboard with a picture of a thin body, places it in front of herself, and joins* JUDY.)

Jeanne   Judy, dear, I know it's none of my business, but if you'd stop eating those great big plates of spaghetti, you could look like this. (*Turns over* JUDY'S *cardboard, which has a thin figure painted on the other side.*)

Judy   Jeanne, dear, I have no desire to look like this. I'm very happy looking like this—(*turning back to fat picture*) There's more to me.

Jeanne   But you'd look so much better if you were a little thinner. (*Turns* JUDY'S *cardboard to thin picture.* JUDY *turns cardboard back to fat side.*)

Judy   But I feel so much better a little fatter.

Jeanne   (*Turning* JUDY'S *cardboard back to thin side*) It's not how you feel, it's how you look!

Judy   (*Turning her cardboard defiantly*) It's not how you look, it's how you feel!

Jeanne   Oh, Judy, you could be such a winner, if you were a little thinner.

Judy   I'm very glad I'm fat, and that is that.

(DOUG *carries a cardboard painted with a thin body in front of him.*)

Doug
Thin thin thin thin
Thin thin thin thin
Thin thin thin thin
THIN!

(IRVING *carries a cardboard with a picture of a fat body.*)

Irving
Fat fat fat fat
Fat fat fat fat
Fat fat fat fat
FAT!

Doug and Jeanne
Thin thin thin thin
Thin thin thin thin
Thin thin thin thin
THIN!

Judy and Irving
Fat fat fat fat
Fat fat fat fat
Fat fat fat fat
FAT!

Doug and Jeanne   We like it our way.

Judy and Irving   We like it our way.

All   Most people only like what they've been taught.

Judy   Wait a minute. I want an outside opinion. (*She points to her cardboard body and turns to audience.*) Don't you think this is the best way to look?

(Audience says Yes and No.)

Jeanne   And I would like an outside opinion. (*Points to her cardboard and turns to audience.*) Don't you think this is the best way to look?

(Audience says Yes and No.)

Doug   Remember that song?

Jeanne   What song?

Doug   That song.

Irving   The song you made up.

Doug   I did not make up that song.

Jeanne   That's the song everybody knows.

Judy   Everybody does not know that song.

Irving   Why argue when we can sing that song?

All
Everybody, Everybody, Everybody, Everybody,
Everybody thinks they're doing it right.

(Repeat.)

Judy   (*Leaning to* IRVING's *ear*) Irving, I don't care what they say, I'm still in the mood for a great big plate of spaghetti.

(Action music. JUDY and IRVING dance around stage. JEANNE and DOUG put down their cardboard costumes. IRVING and JUDY put down cardboards. Music ends.)

Ready to Fight

JEANNE hands DOUG a pair of cardboard boxing gloves. DOUG, wearing cardboard gloves, does some shadow boxing. IRVING walks across stage reading a book. He laughs at something he is reading. DOUG thinks IRVING is laughing at him. DOUG tries to ignore IRVING, but finally socks him on jaw. IRVING falls to floor and then rises.

Doug Anybody who laughs at me gets socked.

Irving Douglas, what is troubling you?

Doug Oh, so you want to fight, huh?

(JUDY and JEANNE have been looking on. Now they rush to DOUG and IRVING.)

Judy A fight, a fight!

Irving I was just walking along, reading my book, and Douglas came along and socked me on the jaw.

Judy   Sock him back, Irving.

Doug   Come on, Irving, sock me back.

Jeanne   Calm down.

Judy   (*To* IRVING) Go ahead and hit him.

Doug   Go ahead and hit me, Irving.

Jeanne   Talk it over.

Irving   We could talk it over, Douglas.

Judy   Don't be a coward, Irving.

Doug   (*Taunting*) Don't be a coward.

Irving   Coward! (*Slams book shut. To* JUDY) What do you mean, don't be a coward? How would you like it if someone came along and socked you on your pretty little jaw? You wouldn't like it, would you? (To DOUG) And as for you, don't you have a brain in that little head of yours? Well, use it! It's people like you who are causing crime in the streets. It's people like you who are causing wars in this world, and it's people like you who can't relate to people like me and . . .

Doug   (*Collapses on floor*) You ought to be ashamed of yourself!

Jeanne   (*To* IRVING) Look what you did!

Judy   He's flat on his back.

Doug   (*Rising slightly*) Irving Burton, you shouldn't have done that to me.

Irving   Well, Douglas, I fight with words. Come on, don't be sore. Remember that song?

Doug   What song?

Judy   That song.

Irving   The song you made up.

Doug   I did not make up that song.

Jeanne   That's the song everybody knows.

Judy   Everybody does not know that song.

Irving   (*Throwing book in air*) Why argue when we can sing that song?

(*The entire cast dances and rolls hands.*)

All
Everybody, Everybody, Everybody, Everybody,
Everybody thinks they're doing it right.

(*Repeat.*)

(*All shake hands and exit on action music.*)

The Chicken
and the Egg

PROPS

white turtleneck sweaters   paper-cone noses
belts   eyeglasses
tails made of newspaper strips

PRODUCTION NOTES

This play is easily adapted for groups of any size. Big EGGS and small
CHICKENS or small EGGS and big CHICKENS are equally humorous. Oversized white turtleneck sweaters with neck openings worn
around head and caught under chin make good EGG costumes.
EGGS' arms should remain folded during skit. Paper cones attached to
heavy-rimmed eyeglasses make funny CHICKEN faces. Newspapers
cut in strips and attached to a belt can be used for CHICKEN tails.

CHICKENS   EGGS

The Chicken and the Egg

All the EGGS *are on one side of the stage. All the* CHICKENS *are on the other side of the stage.* 1ST EGG *and* 1ST CHICKEN *rush to center of stage.*

1st Egg   I was here first.

1st Chicken   I was here first.

1st Egg   I was here first.

1st Chicken   I was here first.

1st Egg   I was here first.

1st Egg and 1st Chicken   *(Sing)*
All my life I've been in doubt.
Won't you please help me out?

Which came first?
The chicken or the egg,
Or the egg or the chicken
Or the chicken or the egg?

(1ST EGG *and* 1ST CHICKEN *rejoin their friends. There is a hubbub of talk in each group.* 2ND CHICKEN *and* 2ND EGG *rush to center of stage.*)

2nd Egg   I was here first.

2nd Chicken   I was here first.

2nd Egg   I beg your pardon.

2nd Chicken   I beg your pardon.

2nd Egg and 2nd Chicken   (*Sing*)
All my life I've been in doubt.
Won't you please help me out?

All
Which came first?
The chicken or the egg,
Or the egg or the chicken
Or the chicken or the egg?

(*All* CHICKENS *and all* EGGS *rush excitedly around the stage. Each* CHICKEN *finds an* EGG *and in pairs they argue.*)

3rd Chicken
How can there be any doubt?
If you didn't have a chicken,
An egg couldn't come out!

4th Chicken
Where do you think you would be?
Without me you wouldn't be.

5th Chicken   Anybody can see that I came first. There's more to me than there is to you. I have a beak. I have wings and feathers. You're nothing but a blank empty shape.

3rd Egg   Who needs all those foolish feathers, anyway? I'll have you know I'm the basic original shape. It's simple, it's beautiful, and it works.

1st Chicken   What are you talking about? I know much more than you because I'm older than you. I've been an egg; you've never been a chicken.

1st Egg   Which proves my point. You've been an egg, which shows you that an egg came first.

2nd Egg   Eggsactly.

2nd Chicken   But, but, but, but you had to come from something, like perhaps maybe a chicken.

All Chickens   Cluck. Cluck.

4th Egg   Well, it certainly gives you something to think about.

All   (*Sing and dance*)
All my life I've been in doubt.
Won't you please help me out?

Which came first?
The chicken or the egg,
Or the egg or the chicken
Or the chicken or the egg?

4th Egg   I don't care what those birdbrains say, I feel first.

3rd Egg   I feel first too; way down deep in my yolk, I feel first.

1st Chicken   Listen, don't listen to those brainless creatures.

2nd Chicken   I don't take them seriously. They're cracked.

Eggs   I was here first.

Chickens   I was here first.

All
All my life I've been in doubt.
Won't you please help me out?

Which came first?
The chicken or the egg,
Or the egg or the chicken
Or the chicken or the egg?

(Entire cast exits quarreling and cackling.)

Big Burger

PROPS

TREE
car
ROAD
lollipop
SIGN with Big Burger on one
   side, Frozen Custard on the
   other

Big Burger, a huge ball of white
   paper with tiny cardboard
   hamburger wrapped inside
hats for MOTHER, FATHER,
   and CHILD

PRODUCTION NOTES

TREE is a cardboard cutout. An actor stands behind it, holding it. The car is made of the sides of a large cardboard box without top and bottom. Three actors barely fit into it. It is painted a bright color with four wheels and a door that actually opens and has Velcro to keep it closed. To move, the actors hold the car up slightly above the ground and walk. The ROAD is a flat piece of painted cardboard, painted with a road in a countryside, about 8 by 6 feet. It is braced to remain stiff when it turns and has hand holes to enable the person behind it to manipulate it. The stage floor is marked with tape, so that the ROAD knows where to stop and turn. The SIGN, a piece of cardboard about 30 inches square, has a hamburger on one side and a frozen custard on the other. It is carried by an actor. If the actor is short, the sign can be put on a stick, so it can pop up above the ROAD flat. Lollipop is a cardboard circle glued onto a tongue depressor. Big Burger is a huge ball made up of 3 feet of white wrapping paper wound around itself. For Big Burger's voice, an offstage voice spoken into a microphone is dramatic. If this is not possible, a hole should be cut in ROAD, so the voice of Big Burger can be heard through the flat.

26

Big Burger

Action music. Enter TREE. *It stops halfway across stage. Enter* MOTHER, FATHER, *and* CHILD *in car.* FATHER *is driving.* MOTHER *and* CHILD, *who is holding a cardboard lollipop, are looking at the countryside. Music ends.*

Mother   Well, here we are, on the outskirts of our very own town, ready at last to start our big trip across the country.

Child   Ma, Pa, how far is it to the Grand Canyon?

Father   It's a long way off.

Mother   But first we have to get to the open road. Step on the gas.

Father   We're off!

(Action music. Enter the ROAD. *It goes in a direction opposite to the car, giving the feeling that the car is traveling. Suddenly* BIG BURGER SIGN *pops up above the* ROAD. *The car stops. Music ends.)*

Sign   *(With booming voice)* Big Burger.

Child   Ma, there's a talking sign.

Sign   *(With booming voice)* Get your Big Burger!

Mother   It is, it's a talking sign.

Child   Could we have a Big Burger for lunch?

Mother   You just had breakfast.

Child   But I love Big Burgers.

Father   I'll tell you what— Let's start the trip off with a treat. Besides, I'm hungry myself.

(Action music. Car and ROAD *again pass each other.* ROAD *turns upside down.* SIGN *again pops up above road. Car stops. Music ends.)*

Child   Goody.

Sign   Big Burger.

Mother   I'm not going up that hill.

Father   Well, why did we buy this new car, if we can't climb up a little hill?

28

Child   Besides, Ma, the Grand Canyon has bigger hills than that.

Mother   All right, you can go up it, but I'm not looking.

(*Action music. Car slants as if going uphill, then jerks as if stalling. Family argues.* ROAD *suddenly switches position. Car lurches forward.* BIG BURGER SIGN *disappears. Music ends.*)

Father   Now where did that Burger go?

Mother   This whole thing is a wild-goose chase.

Child   But I want a Big Burger.

Mother   Do you want a Big Burger or do you want the Grand Canyon?

(SIGN *reappears above road.*)

Sign   (*With booming voice*) Big Burger!

(*Action music.* ROAD *with* SIGN *on top of it moves from one side of stage to another.* SIGN *disappears behind* ROAD. *Car follows at top speed.* ROAD *spins, car spins.* ROAD *crosses stage, with car following wildly.*)

Father   Where is it?

Mother   The other way.

Child   You missed it.

Mother   Turn around.

Father   I can't see where I'm going.

Child   I'm getting sick.

(*Car and* ROAD *come to a sudden halt.* SIGN *disappears behind* ROAD. *Music ends.*)

Sign   You are here!

Family   We're here.

Father   (*Holding door of car open for child*) Come on, darling. Get out, angel.

(*Family stands facing* ROAD.)

Sign   Your hamburger dream has come true!

(*A huge round white paper package comes up from behind* ROAD. *Family reaches for it and gently places it on the floor.*)

Mother   It's bigger than I thought.

Father   It sure is big.

Child   I want it! I want it!

(*Big Burger Waltz. Family unwraps package and spreads paper across the floor. As they continue to unwrap the package they begin to dance, throwing the paper in the air. The stage is soon covered with yards and yards of white paper.* FATHER *finally completely unrolls it and finds a very small cardboard burger. Music ends.)*

Father   Here it is.

Mother   Is this our hamburger dream come true?

Father   Some surprise.

Mother   *(To* CHILD*)* Here, dear, you take it.

*(*CHILD *takes a bite and cries loudly.* MOTHER *also starts to cry.)*

Father   Come on, dear, let's get out of here.

Mother   What are we going to do with all this paper? We can't just leave it on the highway. Let's pick it up and take it with us.

*(*CHILD *gets into car.* MOTHER *and* FATHER *pick up paper and stuff it into car, completely covering* CHILD. MOTHER *and* FATHER *settle into car without noticing* CHILD *is covered with paper.)*

Child   I can't breathe.

Mother   That's all right, dear.

*(*CHILD *pushes paper away from her face.)*

Mother   Now let's cheer up. Let's start this whole trip all over again.

Child   Now how far is it to the Grand Canyon?

Father   Oh, it's a long way off.

Sign   (*With booming voice*) Frozen custard! (*Pops up.*)

Child   Frozen Custard!

Mother   Now that sounds good.

Father   Let's get it!

Child   I want it! I want it!

(*Action music. The* ROAD *with the* FROZEN CUSTARD SIGN *exits. The car lurches forward and follows with the family shouting.*)

PROPS

blackboard made of cardboard
chalk
books
paper money

coins
handkerchief
long cardboard box
milk crate

PRODUCTION NOTES

The blackboard is a large piece of reinforced cardboard, painted black and made to be self-standing. ALLIGATOR's costume is a long rectangular cardboard box that sits on the actor's head. Cut a zigzag line along the long sides of box, making a jagged mouth. The back side of the box is scored so it acts as a hinge. A hole in bottom of box is for actor's head. There are hand holes in middle of top and bottom of box, so the actor can open and close mouth. A 12-inch-long tail, made of small pieces of cardboard taped together, is attached to back of box.

CAST

TEACHER	**BETTY BEATSALL**, a student
MUSIC TEACHER	**ALLIGATOR**

That's Good, That's Good

TEACHER *comes onstage carrying blackboard, sets it down.*

Teacher (*To audience*) There's been a lot of talk about schools and methods these days, so let me tell you right now, I am an old-fashioned teacher. There are many ways to teach—open classes, creative classes, ungraded classes—but I believe in the blackboard. Not only that, I believe in grades. I think that good students should be praised highly. In fact, whenever we hear a correct answer, we all sing.
That's good, that's good,
That's very, very good.
That's good, that's good,
That's very, very good.

35

(The MUSIC TEACHER, *sitting on the side of the stage, accompanies song.)*

Teacher   Today is examination day, and Miss Betty Beatsall, one of my favorite students, will take her exam.

(BETTY BEATSALL *rushes in, carrying a load of books and a milk crate, which she sits on. She jams her books down on the floor and turns pages frantically.)*

Teacher   All right, dear, put down your books and let's get started.

(BETTY *continues to look at her books.)*

Teacher   Put down your book. (BETTY *drops book on pile.)* Thank you, Betty. Now, let's begin. The first test will be in history. I will give you ten seconds and no more to tell me who discovered America. Go!

(TEACHER *is absorbed in looking at his watch. He has his back to* BETTY. BETTY *rushes down to audience and covers side of her mouth, so* TEACHER *will not hear.)*

Betty   (*In stage whisper*) I can't remember! Who discovered America?

Audience   Columbus.

Betty   What's his full name?

Audience   Christopher Columbus.

Teacher Time is up, Betty Beatsall.

(BETTY *goes to her seat.*)

Teacher Who discovered America?

Betty (*Proudly*) Christopher Columbus.

Teacher That's good! (*To audience*) Tell her.

Teacher and Audience
That's good, that's good,
That's very, very good.
That's good, that's good,
That's very, very good.

Teacher Very good, Betty. *A* in history. (*Writes* A *on blackboard.*) Very good, very good. And now we come to my favorite subject—spelling. I will give you five seconds and no more to tell me—How do you spell cat? Go!

(TEACHER *looks at his watch with his back to* BETTY *and she rushes downstage to audience.*)

Betty (*In stage whisper*) How do you spell cat?

Audience C-A-T.

Teacher All right, time is up, Betty.

(BETTY *returns to her seat.*)

Teacher   How do you spell cat?

Betty   *(Proudly)* C-A-T.

TEACHER *writes another* A *on blackboard.*

Teacher and Audience   *(Sing)*
That's good, that's good.
That's very, very good.
That's good, that's good.
That's very, very good.

Teacher   Another A, Betty. That is excellent, excellent. Frankly, I am very surprised. I am completely over-whelmed. Wonderful, Betty. And now we come to the final test of all—arithmetic. I will give you one second and no more to tell me how much one plus one is. Go!

*(*BETTY *rushes to audience as* TEACHER *concentrates on his watch with his back to* BETTY.*)*

Betty   *(In stage whisper)* How much is one plus one?

Audience   Two.

Teacher   Time! How much is one plus one?

Betty   *(Very proud)* One plus one is two.

Teacher
That's good, that's good,
That's very, very good.

That's good, that's good,
That's very, very good.

Teacher (*Writes an* A *on blackboard.*) *A A A*—that is excellent; very, very good; that's wonderful . . . wait a minute! (*Suddenly suspicious.*) Nobody could be that smart. Has someone been helping you?

Betty (*Quietly*) Yes, Mr. Burton.

Teacher Yes, Betty Beatsall? (*Erases the* A*'s on black-board.*) I'm sorry, but I am forced, literally forced, to change your mark to— (*Draws an* F *on blackboard.*) You know what that means: F for failure. Now, who has been helping you?

Betty (*Gestures toward audience.*) All my friends have been helping me. (*Points to audience.*)

Teacher (*To audience*) Have you been helping Betty with the answers?

(*Audience says Yes.*)

Teacher You have. Well, that's really very nice of you, very nice. But, Betty dear, what are you going to do when you're old and gray and you have to figure out for yourself how much one and one is? What are you going to do?

(BETTY *shakes her head.*)

39

Teacher   What are you going to do?

Betty   I don't know, Mr. Burton, I just don't know.

Teacher   Betty, I am very disappointed in you. (*Starts to cry. He takes out his handkerchief and blows his nose.*) I don't think I can teach you anymore. I'm leaving this room.

(*There is a roar offstage. A huge* ALLIGATOR *enters. He chases the teacher and* BETTY *around the room. He corners the* TEACHER.)

Teacher   What are you?

Alligator   I am an alligator.

Teacher   What do you want?

Alligator   I just escaped from the zoo and I need twelve dollars and fifty-nine cents for bus fare back to the Everglades.

Teacher   Twelve dollars and fifty-nine cents for bus fare back to the Everglades?

Alligator   Yes, you heard me. (*Opens his mouth wide and threatens* TEACHER.)

Betty   Alligator, can I have five minutes?

(ALLIGATOR *growls.*)

Betty   Just five minutes.

Alligator   Yes.

Betty   (*Whispering to cornered teacher*) Mr. Burton, have you got the money?

Teacher   No.

(ALLIGATOR *growls again, threatening* TEACHER.)

Teacher   Wait, wait, wait, here is my last ten dollars.

Betty   Ten dollars from twelve fifty-nine. That still leaves two fifty-nine.

Teacher   That's good, that's good, that's—

(ALLIGATOR *growls louder.*)

Betty   Mr. Burton, we need more money.

(TEACHER *and* STUDENT *are huddled together.* ALLIGATOR *is towering over them.*)

Teacher   All right, Betty, I'll ask Mr. Ashwander, the music teacher. Stay here. (*Tiptoes in front of* ALLIGATOR *to* MUSIC TEACHER. *Pianist takes money from his pocket.*)

Teacher   Thank you, Mr. Ashwander, you've saved our lives. Thank you. (*Tiptoes back in front of* ALLIGATOR, *who growls as he passes him.*) Don't you breathe on me, you crocodile! Here, Betty, is two dollars and fifty cents. Ten dollars . . . and two dollars and fifty cents.

Betty (*Counts money*) And I have nine cents, which makes twelve dollars and fifty-nine cents!

Teacher That's good.

Alligator Give it here.

Teacher Go ahead, dear. Don't be afraid. He's really very gentle. (*Pushes* BETTY *toward* ALLIGATOR. BETTY'S *entire body is trembling as she extends her arm and finally throws money into* ALLIGATOR'S *mouth.*)

Alligator Thanks a lot. I'll send you the money back as soon as I get home. (*Exits leaping.*)

Teacher Betty, do you know you're very smart?

Betty I am?

Teacher You are very smart. And do you know what? For courage and intelligence, and most of all for fast thinking, I am going to change your grades to A for excellent.

Betty (*Looks at blackboard*) That's good. (*To audience*) Tell him!

(BETTY *and audience repeat* song.)

(BETTY *and* TEACHER *exit, carrying books and black-board.*)

Ma and the Kids

PROPS

cardboard box for table
milk crate for MA to sit on
broom
dish towel
bag of potato chips
bowl
plastic ketchup containers
plastic water glasses
salt shaker
sheet
tie
shoes
shirt

belt
sneakers
notebook
report card
gym suit
hockey stick
lunch box
violin case
apron for MA
boxes for CHILDREN and
    MA to sit on
plant
cardboard dishes
alarm clock

PRODUCTION NOTES

"Ma and the Kids" is written for a cast of four. It may be adapted for any number by adding more children to the family. MA should wear a large apron. Oversized clothing on CHILDREN creates a humorous effect.

CAST

MA   BETTY
JUDY   IRVING

Ma and the Kids

MA *is onstage tidying house. In run* BETTY, JUDY, *and* IRVING. *They stand in the center of stage, looking proud.* MA *stops her work, smiles at her children and walks toward them.*

Ma (*To audience*) This is Betty, the most intelligent child in her class. This is Judy, a real little lady. And this is Irving. He's the hero of his class, and he's my hero too.

Children And that's our Ma, the best Ma in the whole wide world. Ma, we're hungry!

Ma Well, children, set the table.

(CHILDREN *race out, then reenter, bringing table. They sit behind table.* MA *sits at head of table.*)

45

Ma I didn't have time to shop, so we're going to have—

Children Potato chips!

Ma (*Stands and empties potato chips into large bowl.*) Right! (*Starts to sit down.*)

Betty Ma, may I please have some ketchup?

Ma Of course. (*Action music. Exits and returns with bottle of ketchup.*)

Judy Ma, may I have some salt?

Ma Oh, I forgot the salt. (*Exits and returns with salt shaker.*)

Irving Ma, there's no water.

Ma Oh, isn't there any water? (*Exits and returns with glass of water.*)

Betty I need more ketchup, please.

Ma You do love ketchup. (*Begins to run back and forth, moving faster and faster.*)

Judy Guess what, Ma? The salt shaker is empty.

Ma And I just filled it this morning. (*Continues to run back and forth, bringing in more ketchup bottles, salt shakers, and glasses of water.*)

Irving I need more water.

Betty I need more ketchup.

Judy I need more salt.

Irving Water.

Betty Ketchup.

Judy Salt.

Irving Water!

Ma (*Finally sitting down. Music ends.*) Now, children, please pass me some potato chips.

Children Oh, Ma, there aren't any left.

Ma (*Sighs*) Children, clear the table.

(CHILDREN *exit, taking table.*)

Ma (*To audience*) My children do have big appetites, and they sometimes get a little noisy, but when they sleep they're angels.

(*Enter* CHILDREN *standing behind sheet, which they hold under their chins. They stand still with eyes closed.* MA *closes her eyes. Alarm clock goes off.*)

Ma (*To* CHILDREN) Children, it's time to get up. The birds are up. The bees are up. The sun is up. Everything is up, up, up, up, up.

(CHILDREN *adjust covers, mumble, and continue to sleep.*)

Ma   Children, the birds are up, the bees are up, the insects are up, the flowers are up. It's time to get up. (*Looks at watch.*) It's eight twenty-nine! The school bus will be here in one minute!

(CHILDREN *toss sheet away frantically.*)

Irving   That's my sweater!

Judy   That's my shoe!

Betty   I can't find my belt.

Irving   Who has my shirt?

Judy   Has anybody seen my eyeglasses?

All   Good-bye, Ma.

(*Exit* CHILDREN.)

Ma   Just a little tidying up to do, and then I'll have a nice, quiet day all to myself. (*Starts to sweep. Action music.* JUDY *enters.*)

Judy   Ma, I forgot my sneakers. Can you help me find them?

Ma   Here they are.

Judy   Thanks, Ma. Good-bye, Ma. (*Exits.*)

Ma   Good-bye, dear. Now, what was I doing?

(Each time the CHILDREN *enter, they rush across stage and disappear. They reappear with objects they had forgotten, rush back across stage, and exit.)*

Betty   I forgot my notebook.

Judy   I forgot my report card.

Betty   I forgot my gym suit.

Ma   I'll dry the dishes.

Irving   I forgot my violin.

Judy   I forgot my plant for science class.

Ma   Whoops, I dropped a dish!

Betty   I forgot my hockey stick.

Irving   I forgot my lunch.

Ma   Hurry off to school, dears, or you'll be late. Now, what was I doing?

*(*CHILDREN *enter. By this time they are all loaded down with their school things.)*

Children   Ma, we forgot to kiss you good-bye! (*All kiss* MA *and exit.)*

Ma   (*Calling after them*) Good-bye, dears.

Children (*Offstage*) Good-bye, Ma.

Ma At last I can clean the house. Oh, dear! (*Very loud*) Children, come back!

(*Music ends.* CHILDREN *rush in.*)

Betty What is it?

Irving What happened?

Judy Did I forget something I didn't remember?

Ma I forgot something. Today is Saturday. There's no school.

Children Hurrah! (*They throw their things in the air.* MA *collapses on the floor.*)

Blown Off
the Billboard

PROPS

billboard

paintbrushes

paint cans

rope

drop cloth

extra strips of brown wrapping
   paper for GARBAGE

transistor radio, made of a small
   cardboard box

rags

hat for LITTLE PAINTER

fishing line

red paper poncho

cardboard triangle, painted as
   an ICE CREAM CONE

sheets of brown wrapping paper

PRODUCTION NOTES

Billboard is a heavy piece of cardboard, about 6 by 5 feet, with a lip-shaped hole in the middle. A red paper is taped to back of cardboard, over the hole. Paper must be replaced for every performance. The paper is lightly scored so LIPS can break through easily. An advertisement for lipstick is painted on the front of the billboard, above and below the hole. LIPS' costume is a paper poncho with a liplike shape painted red. GARBAGE wears large, floor-length sheets of brown wrapping paper, wrinkled, torn, and spotted, which are tied at the neck. ICE CREAM CONE is a cardboard triangle painted light brown. A fishing line attached to LITTLE PAINTER's hat pulled by someone offstage gives the effect of the wind blowing off the hat. A PROP PERSON hidden behind the billboard and moving it gives the illusion of wind blowing the billboard. The PROP PERSON must disappear before PAINTERS drop billboard.

CAST

BIG PAINTER   ICE CREAM CONE
LITTLE PAINTER   GARBAGE
LIPS   PROP PERSON

Blown Off the Billboard

Action music. Two SIGN PAINTERS, *one big, one little, run onto the stage. They are holding a billboard. The billboard is being tossed by the wind and the painters are having trouble holding it. They are also holding paintbrushes, paint cans, some rags, and a drop cloth. The character* LIPS *is hidden behind the sign.*

Big Painter   What a wind! Hey, give me a hand.

Little Painter   (*His hat is blown off and he runs after it, leaving other painter holding billboard.*) Look, there goes my hat.

Big Painter   Would you get the billboard, please?

Little Painter   But I'll lose my hat!

Big Painter   I've got it. (*Catches hat. Lets go of billboard.*)

53

Little Painter   Get the sign. . . .

Big Painter   Got it. Come on, hold on.

Little Painter   I can't.

(Sign is blown back and forth. LIPS *breaks through as sign and* PAINTERS *fall to the ground. Music ends.)*

Lips   Whew! Blown right off the billboard! Or did you two fellows knock me off? Hey, I'm talking. I'm walking. I'm a talking, walking pair of lips.

*(*PAINTERS *scramble to feet and hold up broken sign.)*

Big Painter   Hey, would you please get back on there?

Lips   Get back on where, sir?

Little Painter   Back on that billboard.

Big Painter   Yeah, the billboard.

Lips   I couldn't possibly get back on that tattered old thing.

Big Painter   Oh, come on, now, be reasonable. You can't go walking around the city streets.

Lips   Walking around the city streets! That's what I'd like to do.

Little Painter   Don't listen to her. We could easily grab her and put her back up there.

Big Painter   Good idea. Hey, come back here!

Lips   I am not getting back on that billboard.

Big Painter   Listen, you don't want a couple of nice guys like us to lose our jobs, do you?

Lips   Well, no, I don't want anybody to get in trouble on account of me.

Little Painter   Look, Lips, why don't you let us just put you back up there, where you belong?

Lips   But it's uncomfortable. I don't even fit anymore.

Big Painter   We'll use some extra glue.

Lips   Look, I don't want to get back on that billboard before I have an adventure. I thought that maybe I could meet another pair of lips or maybe even an ice cream cone.

Big Painter   An ice cream cone? Walking around the city streets? Ha, ha, ha.

(The two painters laugh. Enter ICE CREAM CONE, *singing.)*

Ice Cream Cone
Tutti frutti, what a cutie,
Creamy rich and so delicious.
La, la, la, la, la, la, la, la, la, la, la, la.

Yummy, yummy, yummy, yummy,
It's so good inside your tummy.
An ice cream cone, an ice cream cone—
That's me!

(Exits.)

Lips What did I tell you? Ice Cream Cone, come back!

Little Painter Look, Lips, we've got to get you back on this billboard.

Lips Well, you're going to have to catch me first. *(Runs offstage.)*

Painters Hey, come back here! (*Action music.* PAINTERS *run after* LIPS, *carrying billboard.*)

(On runs GARBAGE. *He runs around the stage as if pursued, looking over his shoulder. He throws himself on the floor, in a mound.* LIPS *enters and throws herself on top of* GARBAGE. *Enter painters, holding billboard.)*

Little Painter I'm sure they came this way.

Big Painter Those lips have got to be here someplace.

Little Painter We've got to find them.

Big Painter Let's keep looking.

Little Painter Okay.

(Sign painters exit. Music ends.)

Garbage   Hey, get off me!

Lips   Oh, what did I sit on?

Garbage   What are you?

Lips   I'm a pair of lips, blown off a billboard. But what in the world are you?

Garbage   I'm a bag of garbage. Can't you tell? They threw me out into the street two weeks ago.

Lips   What are you doing here?

Garbage   I ran away. They've been chasing me ever since.

Lips   Boy, you must be tired, running all that time.

Garbage   It's not so bad. All you need is a little music.

Lips   Where in this city do you find music?

Garbage   Just the other day a transistor radio came sailing out of a window, and I've been using it ever since. All you have to do is find a station with a good beat and turn it on.

(He pulls out a transistor radio, hidden in his costume. He turns a knob on the radio. Action music. GARBAGE dances and is joined by LIPS. Music ends.)

57

Lips   Boy, is it fun to run to music!

Garbage   See, what did I tell you?

Painters   (*Offstage*) There they are.

Lips   It's those sign painters again. What'll I do? Where'll I go?

Garbage   Run down the street.

Lips   Which way?

Garbage   (*Points*) That way.

Lips   Garbage, you won't forget about me, will you?

Garbage   No, go!

(*Exit* LIPS. GARBAGE *throws himself on the ground, looking like a mound. Enter sign painters.*)

Little Painter   Those lips have got to be here somewhere.

Big Painter   (*Looking at* GARBAGE) What is that?

Little Painter   (*Sniffs*) G A R B A G E !

Big Painter   Get rid of it.

Little Painter   (*Pushes* GARBAGE *offstage.*) Let's figure out what to do.

Big Painter   Listen, if I see those lips, I'll lasso them with my rope.

Little Painter   And I'll slap them all over with paste.

Big Painter   And then we'll stick them up against the sign. And we'll press them down so tight they'll never get away.

Little Painter   But they're not here.

Big Painter   What we need is something to lure them out.

Little Painter   We need something so delicious those lips can't resist it.

Big Painter   What we need is that ice cream cone.

(Enter ICE CREAM CONE, *singing.)*

Ice Cream Cone
Tutti frutti, what a cutie,
Creamy rich and so delicious.
La, la, la, la, la, la, la, la, la, la, la, la.
Yummy, yummy, yummy, yummy,
It's so good inside your tummy.
An ice cream cone, an ice cream cone—
That's me!

Little Painter   Ice Cream, may I tell you something?

Ice Cream Cone   Sure.

Little Painter   You have a beautiful voice.

Ice Cream Cone   Thank you.

Big Painter   Ice Cream Cone, can I tell you something else?

Ice Cream Cone   Of course.

Big Painter   You are my favorite flavor.

Ice Cream Cone   (*Flattered and embarrassed*) Thank you very much.

Little Painter   Ice Cream Cone, may I ask you a favor?

Ice Cream Cone   Anything.

Little Painter   Would you sing that song again?

Big Painter   We could listen to that song again and again.

Ice Cream Cone   (*Sings*)
Tutti frutti, what a cutie,
Creamy rich and so delicious.
La, la, la, la, la, la, la, la, la, la, la, laaaa.
Yummy, yummy, yummy, yummy,
It's so good inside your tummy.
An ice cream cone, an ice cream cone—
That's me!

How's that?

Little Painter   Beautiful.

Big Painter   Sing it again.

Ice Cream Cone
  Tutti frutti, what a cutie,
  Creamy rich and so delicious.

(Enter LIPS, *singing.)*

Lips
  Yummy, yummy, yummy, yummy,
  It's so good inside my tummy.
  An ice cream cone, an ice cream cone,
  For me.

Ice Cream Cone   Who are you?

(SIGN PAINTERS *start creeping up behind* LIPS *and* ICE CREAM CONE.)

Lips   I'm a pair of lips blown off a billboard, and I've been an admirer of yours for a long, long time. I'm so pleased to be finally meeting you.

Ice Cream Cone   Well, I'm very happy to meet you.

(SIGN PAINTERS *throw a drop cloth over* LIPS *and* ICE CREAM CONE *and pull them down to the ground.)*

Painters   We've got 'em.

Lips and Ice Cream Cone (*Under cloth, shouting*) Garbage, help!

(GARBAGE *enters. Action music. He waves strips of paper in the air, threatening* PAINTERS. *Hurls himself at* PAINTERS *and chases them around stage. They drop their brushes and pails.* GARBAGE, *jumping and whirling, follows them as they exit. Music ends.*)

Lips and Ice Cream Cone Hurrah for Garbage!

(GARBAGE *returns.*)

Lips Garbage, you saved us. Oh, I'd like you to meet a friend of mine. Ice Cream Cone, meet Garbage.

Ice Cream Cone Garbage, you're a real hero.

Garbage Thank you. But look, Lips, we're not safe yet. Those two won't be satisfied until you're back on that billboard.

Lips Oh, dear, where can we go? Where can we hide?

Garbage We can go anywhere—Pittsburgh, St. Louis, Detroit, Chicago. They've got garbage everywhere.

Lips Ice Cream, will you come with us?

Ice Cream Cone I'd love to go, but it's a long way to Chicago.

Lips Look, Garbage, have you still got that radio?

Garbage   Sure. (*Turns radio on.*)

(*Music starts.* LIPS *and* GARBAGE *start to do a running dance step.* ICE CREAM CONE *is intrigued, joins the dance.*)

Lips   We'll be in Chicago in no time.

(*Action music. All exit, dancing.*)

PROPS

newspaper
2 derby hats
2 cardboard autos
cardboard ax
milk crate painted gray for
    pedestal

a tall cardboard box for
    BUILDING
2 horns for autos
business suit for MAYOR
business suit for GOVERNOR
gray cloth

PRODUCTION NOTES

The two cardboard automobiles are made of large cardboard boxes with swinging doors cut out so that actors can climb in and out. A horn is attached to the side of each auto. The BUILDING is made of a tall cardboard box with small squares cut out for windows. The actor holds the box so legs show and looks through a large cutout square at face level. The STATUE wears gray material draped over shoulders, which reaches to pedestal. Scenery consists of a large (9 feet high by 10 feet wide) paper or cardboard painting of city buildings. Two prop people stand behind the painting and hold it up with poles attached to the top.

The Building and the Statue

CAST

BUILDING   MAYOR
STATUE   GOVERNOR
MAN

The Building and the Statue

Entrance music. A large painting of a city slowly comes across stage. STATUE, *carrying milk crate, and* BUILDING *are behind the painting. When painting reaches center stage, actors behind it stop and* STATUE *climbs on pedestal.* BUILDING *sets itself near* STATUE. STATUE *assumes pose with index finger in the air. Painting exits. Music ends.*

Building Good morning, dear Statue. Isn't it a lovely day?

Statue Good morning, dear Building. I don't think it's such a nice day. It's too windy for me.

Building I daresay you're right. I do feel a terrible draft at my top story.

Statue Building, dear, we're in luck. Here comes a newspaper.

66

Building See if you can read the weather report.

(Enter a MAN *reading a newspaper. He pauses in front of the* STATUE, *who leans slightly to read over his shoulder.* MAN *folds his paper and exits.* STATUE *gasps.)*

Building What's the matter?

Statue There was something in the paper about you.

Building About me? What did it say?

Statue Dear Building, it says they plan to tear you down.

Building That's impossible! They can't do that.

Statue Let's not get too upset. Newspapers often print mistakes.

(Actors and pianist make traffic sounds with kazoos and car horns. Enter MAYOR *in a cardboard car. He makes sounds of a noisy motor with his voice, and drives madly about stage. Stops his car suddenly and climbs out, holding ax.)*

Mayor *(To audience)* Fellow citizens, as Mayor of your fair city, I've come here today to welcome you all to a very important ceremony. Today we are going to start to rebuild our city. Now we all want a modern, up-to-date city, don't we? *(Audience says Yes and No.)* Yes! So today we are going to tear down this old dilapidated building to make way for a highway. And now I, your

67

Mayor, in the name of progress, will strike the first blow! (*Raises ax.*)

Building Why, Irving Burton! I haven't seen you since you were in the third grade.

Mayor Did you hear that? Could it be? Is it possible? Yes, yes, it is! It's the building where I was born. What a beautiful old building this is! This should be a national monument! Wait a minute—we were going to build a highway right through here. I'll just move it over a couple of inches and get rid of this ugly old statue. (*Moves toward* STATUE *and raises ax.*) One, two, three . . .

(*Enter* GOVERNOR.)

Governor Hello, Mayor. How is the ceremony going?

Mayor Governor! I was just getting ready to tear down that ugly old statue.

Governor Why, you can't tear down that statue. That's a statue of me. (GOVERNOR *assumes same pose as* STATUE.)

Mayor (*To audience*) Isn't that an amazing resemblance?

Governor I thought you were going to tear down this ugly dilapidated old building.

Mayor We can't tear down this beautiful old building. This is where I was born. It's a landmark.

Governor Well, we can't tear down that statue. That's a statue of me.

Mayor Governor, we must put a highway through here.

Governor We can't put it here. We'll have to put it over there.

Mayor We cannot touch that building. That's where I was born!

Governor We cannot touch that statue. That's a statue of me!

Mayor I know what I'm going to do.

Governor I know what I'm going to do.

(GOVERNOR *and* MAYOR *get into their cars and drive wildly around stage.*)

Governor I'm going to City Hall, you're not going to get away with this. (*Cars collide.*) You dented my car! What kind of a driver are you?

(GOVERNOR *and* MAYOR *continue driving around stage.*)

Both We've got to tear down something! (*Exit shouting.*)

Building Dear, dear . . . that was nearly the end of us.

Statue I was very frightened for a few minutes.

Building Dear Statue, do you think they'll come back?

69

Statue   I think we'd better leave before they change their minds. Come on. We'll go someplace where they appreciate a nice old building and a good-looking statue.

(STATUE *slowly and heavily steps down from pedestal, picks up pedestal.*)

Building   Someplace high on a hill . . . overlooking a river.

(*Exit music.* STATUE *and* BUILDING *exit, leaving stage empty.*)

PROPS

---

a cardboard BATHTUB
a cardboard MOTHER

a cardboard PETER
a cardboard SOAP

PRODUCTION NOTES

All the costumes are oversized painted pieces of cardboard. Because of their size, they should be braced with wood lathing. Lathing can have hinges or bolts so props can be folded for storage or transport. MOTHER is so large that two people support her. The PETER figure has two sides, clothed in front and nude in back. It also has a hole in it at actor's mouth level through which actor speaks. PETER must be able to bend at knees so it can look as if it were sitting behind tub. The MOTHER's lines, spoken through an offstage microphone turned to loud volume, give a humorous effect. BATHTUB is an actor holding a cardboard cutout. SOAP is an actor on knees so SOAP can look small compared to BATHTUB.

CAST

BATHTUB	**PETER**
SOAP	**MOTHER** (two actors)

I Won't Take a Bath!

Stage is empty. Music. Enter BATHTUB. *He moves with big, clumsy steps. Soap follows.*

Bathtub

I am a bathtub, stalwart and true,
Standing here waiting on the bathroom floor.

Soap

I am a soap bar, firm and square,
And I take my job very seriously.

(Music ends.)

Bathtub and Soap And we're here to give Peter his bath.

Soap Where is that boy?

Bathtub He's in a bad mood.

Soap He hates to take baths.

Bathtub And he's terribly rude.

73

(Enter PETER.)

Peter Are you speaking of me? I heard what you said. I won't take a bath, I'd rather be dead!

Bathtub and Soap *(Sing)*
Oh, please, take a bath,
Oh, please, take a bath,
Oh, please, take a bath today.

Oh, please, take a bath,
Oh, please, take a bath,
Oh, please, take a bath today.

Peter No.

Bathtub and Soap Yes.

Peter. No.

Bathtub and Soap Yeeeeeeessssssss!

Peter *(To audience)* My voice is so little and theirs is so loud. Besides that, it's two against one. I need help. Everyone who hates to take baths, sing with me, "I won't take a bath."

Peter and Audience
I won't take a bath,
I won't take a bath,
I won't take a bath today!

74

I won't take a bath,
I won't take a bath,
I won't take a bath today!

Soap   Well, what'll we do, Tub?

Bathtub   You talk to him, Soap. He'll listen to you.

Soap   Peter, dear Peter, don't you want to be clean?

Peter   Never in my life!

Soap   I told you he wouldn't. He's terribly mean.

Bathtub   (*To audience*) We need help. Mothers and fathers, did you hear what he said?

Soap   He won't take a bath, he'd rather be dead.

Bathtub   Mothers and fathers, you've heard our song.

Soap   Sing along with us, "Oh, please, take a bath today."

Bathtub, Soap, and Audience   (*Sing*)
Oh, please, take a bath,
Oh, please, take a bath,
Oh, please, take a bath today.

Oh, please, take a bath,
Oh, please, take a bath,
Oh, please take a bath today.

Peter   No!

Bathtub and Soap   Yes.

Peter   No.

Bathtub and Soap   Yes.

Peter   No, no, no, no, nooooooo!

Bathtub   (*To audience*) Mothers and fathers and all those who believe in taking baths, sing with us.

Bathtub, Soap and Audience   (*Sing*)
Oh, please, take a bath,
Oh, please, take a bath,
Oh, please, take a bath today.

Oh, please, take a bath,
Oh, please, take a bath,
Oh, please, take a bath today.

Peter   I will never take a bath!

Soap   Wait until your mother comes, young man.

Bathtub   You'll change your tune.

Peter   We'll see about that.

(*Music. Enter* MOTHER.)

Mother   Peter, aren't you in your bath yet? What is taking you so long?

Peter   I was just getting ready, Mother.

(Actor holding PETER *turns figure around so nude side faces audience. He runs behind* BATHTUB *and sets* PETER *down so* PETER *appears to be getting in the* TUB.*)*

Mother   Peter just hates to take baths. Well, I was the same way when I was a child. I even made up a song about it. I think you know the words. Let's all sing.

Actors and Audience   *(Sing)*
   I won't take a bath,
   I won't take a bath,
   I won't take a bath today!

   I won't take a bath,
   I won't take a bath,
   I won't take a bath today!

(Exit BATHTUB *with* PETER *behind it,* SOAP, *and* MOTH-ER.*)*

Everybody, Everybody
action music

Music by
DONALD ASHWANDER

Everybody, Everybody

Words and Music by
DONALD ASHWANDER

Ev - 'ry - bod - y,   ev - 'ry - bod - y,   ev - 'ry - bod - y,   ev - 'ry - bod - y,

ev - 'ry - bod - y thinks they're   do - ing   it   right.   Ev - 'ry - bod - y,   ev - 'ry - bod - y,

ev - 'ry - bod - y,   ev - 'ry - bod - y,   ev - 'ry - bod - y thinks they're   do - ing   it   right.

The Chicken and the Egg

Words by **JUDITH MARTIN**
Music by **DONALD ASHWANDER**

All my life I've been in doubt. Won't you please help me out?

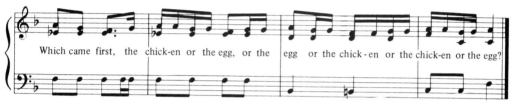

Which came first, the chick-en or the egg, or the egg or the chick-en or the chick-en or the egg?

Big Burger
action music

Music by
DONALD ASHWANDER

Big Burger Waltz

Music by
DONALD ASHWANDER

That's Good, That's Good

Words and Music by
DONALD ASHWANDER

Lively

That's good, that's good, that's ver - y, ver - y good! That's

good, that's good, that's ver - y, ver - y good!

Ma and the Kids
action music

Music by
DONALD ASHWANDER

Blown Off the Billboard
action music

Music by
DONALD ASHWANDER

Ice Cream Song

Words by **IRVING BURTON**
Music by **DONALD ASHWANDER**

Waltz tempo

Tut - ti fruit - ti what a cu - tie.__ Cream-y rich and so de - li - cious.__

La, la, la, la, la, la, la, la, la, la, la, la, la, la, la, la, la, la, la, la.__

Yum-my, yum-my, yum-my, yum - my, __ it's so good in - side your tum - my.__ An

ice cream cone, an ice cream cone, that's me.

The Building and the Statue
entrance music

Music by
DONALD ASHWANDER

exit music

Music by
DONALD ASHWANDER

I Won't Take a Bath!

entrance music

Words and Music by
DONALD ASHWANDER

I Won't Take a Bath!

Music by
DONALD ASHWANDER

Tub and soap: Oh, please take a bath. Oh, please take a bath. Oh,
Peter: I won't take a bath. I won't take a bath. I

please take a bath to - day. _____ Oh,
won't take a bath to - day. _____ I

please take a bath. Oh, please take a bath. Oh,
won't take a bath. I won't take a bath. I

please take a bath to - day.
won't take a bath to - day.

Mother's Entrance

Slowly

About the Author

Judith Martin, the director of The Paper Bag Players, has been a pioneer in creating a new form of children's theater based on a child's everyday experiences and notions of the world. She has written, designed, performed in, and directed twelve original shows, which have all become classics of contemporary children's theater.

The Paper Bag Players have performed to wide acclaim throughout Europe and the United States. The author lives in New York City, headquarters for The Paper Bag Players, with her husband and daughter.

About the Composer

Donald Ashwander has been composing and playing the music for The Paper Bag Players since 1966. His music is known all over the world through both live performances and recordings.

Originally from Alabama, Mr. Ashwander lives and works in New York City.

Gary Ciccati is an art director at an advertising agency. He lives in Bloomfield, New Jersey, with his wife and two young sons.